Why Do Horses Neigh?

by JOAN HOLUB

illustrations by Anna DiVito

PUFFIN BOOKS

PUFFIN BOOKS
Published by the Penguin Group
Penguin Putnam Books for Young Readers, 345 Hudson Street, New York, New York 10014, U.S.A.
Penguin Books Ltd, 80 Strand, WC2R ORL, England
Penguin Books Australia Ltd, Ringwood, Victoria, Australia
Penguin Books Canada Ltd, 10 Alcorn Avenue, Toronto, Ontario, Canada M4V 3B2
Penguin Books (N.Z.) Ltd, 182-190 Wairau Road, Auckland 10, New Zealand

Penguin Books Ltd, Registered Offices: Harmondsworth, Middlesex, England

First published in the United States of America by Dial Books for Young Readers and Puffin
Books, divisions of Penguin Putnam Books for Young Readers, 2003

9 10 8

THE LIBRARY OF CONGRESS HAS CATALOGED THE DIAL EDITION AS FOLLOWS:

Holub, Joan.
Why do horses neigh? / by Joan Holub; illustrations by Anna DiVito.
p. cm.
Summary: Questions and answers present information about the
behavior and characteristics of horses and their interactions with humans.
ISBN 0-8037-2770-4—ISBN 0-14-230119-1 (pbk.)
1. Horses—Miscellanea—Juvenile literature.
[1. Horses—Miscellanea. 2. Human-animal relationships—Miscellanea.
3. Questions and answers.] I. DiVito, Anna, ill. II. Title.
SF302 .H64 2003 636.1—dc21 2001047476

Puffin® and Easy-to-Read® are registered trademarks of Penguin Putnam Inc.

Printed in China
Reading Level 2.4

Photo Credits

Front cover, pages 5, 7, 9, 11 (stripe and bald face horses), 12, 14, 20, 25, 33, 34, 35, 39, 46;
copyright © Dorling Kindersley; pages 1, 11 (trotting roan stallion), 15, 16, 47 copyright ©
Ron Kimball Studios; page 4 copyright © Sandra Seiden; page 8 copyright © Kit Houghton
Photography/ Corbis Images; page 17, 48 copyright © Kathi Lamm/Getty Images; page 18–19
copyright © Jeff Vanuga/Corbis Images; page 29 copyright © Gail Shumway/Getty Images;
page 30 copyright © Rhonda Duewell; page 42 copyright © The Purcell Team/Corbis
Images; page 43 copyright © Jerry Cooke/Corbis Images

Note: Children should be supervised when in the presence of horses.

*For Kristina Duewell, Deborah Kaplan,
and Nick Vitiello*—J.H.

For Cinda, Jenna, and Kate—A.D.

Do you love horses?

Horses are fun to ride.

They make good friends, too.

There are about two hundred kinds,

or breeds, of horses.

Two well-known breeds are

Appaloosa (ap-uh-LOO-suh)

and Arabian (uh-RAY-bee-en).

What are baby and adult horses called?

Horses are called different things
at different ages.

All baby horses are called foals
until they are about one year old.

From one to four years old,
a female horse is called a filly,
and a male horse is called a colt.

A horse is fully grown
by the time it is five years old.
Then it is considered an adult.
An adult female horse
is called a mare.
An adult male horse is called
a stallion.

How is a horse born?

A foal is born after it grows inside

its mother for eleven months.

It is usually born front feet first.

A mother cleans her foal

by licking it all over.

What are foals like?

A foal can stand within one hour

after being born.

Its legs are shaky at first.

But it can run and play

when it is only one day old!

A foal drinks milk from its mother

for the first two months.

Then it begins to nibble grass

and eat horse feed.

When it is about six months old,

a foal stops drinking its mother's milk.

How can people tell their horses apart?

Color and markings are two good
ways to tell horses apart.
Markings are the patches of
white hair on a horse.
Some common head and leg
markings are shown on the next page.

Stripe

Blaze

Bald Face

Star

Coronet   **Pastern**   **Sock**   **Stocking**

What are the different parts of a horse's body called?

The parts of a horse's body are called points.
Some of the main points are the muzzle, mane, withers, and hooves.

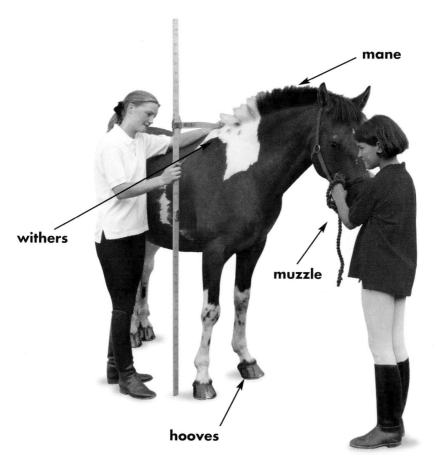

mane

withers

muzzle

hooves

How is a horse measured?

Long ago, the width of a man's hand
was used to measure a horse.
Now a special ruler called
a horse measuring standard is used.
It still uses a hand
as its unit of measurement.
A hand is about four inches long.
Withers are the highest point
on a horse's shoulders.
A horse's height is measured
from its withers to the ground
while it is standing up.
Most horses are about fifteen
or sixteen hands high.

How small is the smallest horse?

Falabella ponies are the smallest horses. They are less than 7.2 hands (30 inches) tall. That's shorter than an average three-year-old child!

How big is the biggest horse?

Shires are the biggest horses.

Some Shires are 21 hands (7 feet) tall

and weigh over two thousand pounds.

That's as much as a small car!

Is a pony a horse?

A pony is any breed of horse that is less than 14.2 hands (58 inches) tall when it is an adult.

Ponies have shorter legs than other horses.

A pony is not a baby horse.

There are many different breeds of ponies. Some well-known breeds are Shetland, Welsh, and Pony of the Americas.

How fast can horses run?

Horses move at four different speeds.

Walking is the slowest speed.

Trotting is running slowly.

Cantering is running a little faster.

Galloping is running as fast as possible.

Many horses can gallop

at a speed of thirty miles an hour.

That is about as fast as a car

drives on a city street.

Most racehorses are

Thoroughbreds (THUR-o-bredz).

They are the fastest horses.

Some Thoroughbreds can run

at speeds of over forty miles an hour.

The fastest people can run only

about sixteen miles an hour.

How can you tell a horse's age?

A horse's teeth show how old it is.
By the age of five, a horse has lost
its twenty-four baby teeth.
It has grown between thirty-six
and forty adult teeth.
As a horse gets older, its teeth
slowly wear down.
The teeth also change color, from
white to yellow, gray, or brown.

How long do horses live?

Horses usually live to be between
twenty and twenty-five years old.
The oldest horse on record,
Old Billy, lived in England.
He lived to be sixty-two years old!

Can horses see better than people can?

You have to turn your head

to look to the side,

but a horse doesn't.

A horse's eyes are on the sides

of its head.

This helps it see in many directions.

Horses also see better at night
than people can.
The back part of a horse's eye
reflects light like a mirror.
This helps it see with only
a tiny bit of light.
Horses do not see colors very well.
They recognize the color yellow best.
A horse's eye is twice as big as your eye.

What does it mean when a horse moves its ears?

Horses can turn their ears

to figure out where a sound

is coming from.

They can hear high and low sounds

that people can't hear.

A horse can also show its feelings

by moving its ears.

If its ears point straight up

and turn far forward,

a horse is interested or surprised.

When its ears are laid back

flat against its head,

it is probably angry or scared.

Why do horses neigh?

Horses neigh to try to find other horses. They are saying, "Hello! I am over here. Are any other horses around?" Since each horse's neigh sounds a little different to another horse, neighs help horses tell one another apart.

What other ways do horses talk?

Horses make a low, soft sound called a nicker to say "Hello." They snort when they are surprised, curious, or worried. A snort is when a horse loudly blows air out of its nose. Horses squeal when they are angry or hurt.

What does it mean when a horse moves its tail?

Horses can also show their feelings
with their tails.

A high tail means a horse
is excited, happy, or full of energy.

A droopy tail means a horse
is unhappy or tired.

A horse may swish its tail
from side to side if it's angry.

Or it may just be shooing away insects!

How do horses get to know each other?

When two horses first meet,

they take turns blowing air

into each other's nose.

That way, the horses get to know

each other by the way they smell.

How much do horses sleep?

Horses sleep about three hours
in a twenty-four-hour day.
They only sleep for about five
minutes at a time.
They can take naps while standing up.
Horses lie down when they want to
sleep more deeply.
A horse sleeps with its eyes shut
just like you do.

What do horses eat?

Horses eat grass, hay,

and special horse feed.

They sometimes like treats

such as pieces of carrot and apple.

Horses can't throw up,

even if they feel sick.

They eat slowly and carefully

so that they don't accidentally eat food

that might make them sick.

Where do horses live?

Horses need to be around
other horses or they get lonely.
Most horses live in buildings
called stables.
A stable is like a barn.

In its stable, each horse has its own small room called a stall. Stalls must be kept clean and dry. Each day, the horse's poop must be removed and clean straw added.

Why do horses wear shoes?

A horse's hooves wear
down as it walks or runs.
Horses wear horseshoes to protect
their hooves from wearing down
or getting hurt.
A metal or rubber shoe is nailed
to the bottom of each hoof.
This does not hurt the horse,
just as it doesn't hurt you
when you cut your toenails.

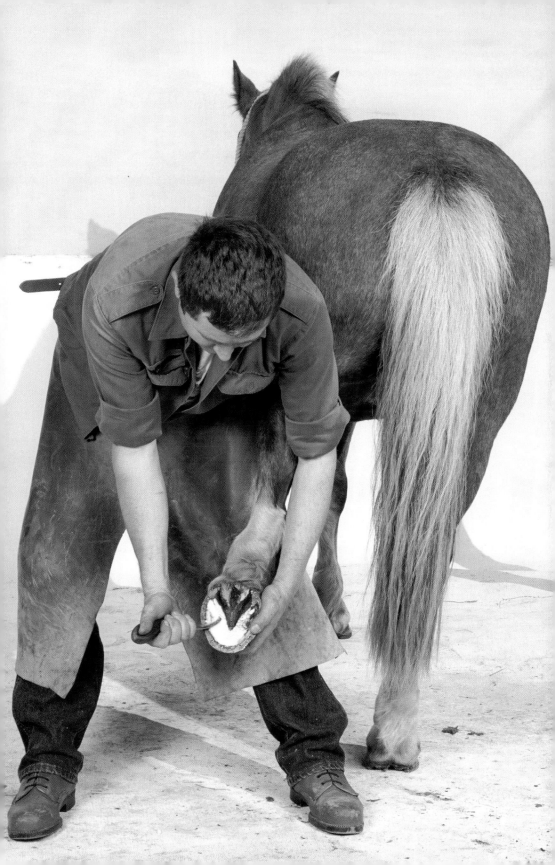

How do horses keep clean?

Horses keep clean by grooming.
Grooming means taking care
of the hair, mane, tail, hooves,
and other parts of a horse.

A horse must be groomed every day.

Horses can do some grooming themselves.

But a horse cannot turn its head

around to clean its own mane

or to reach certain parts of its body.

So horses often help other horses groom

by licking and cleaning one another.

People use special brushes and combs

to clean a horse's coat.

A hoof pick helps remove rocks

and dirt from the hooves.

A horse's eyes and nose

must be cleaned with a sponge.

Taking care of a horse is a lot of work!

What is tack?

A horse's bridle, saddle, and other
equipment used in horseback riding
are called tack.
The bit and reins are part
of the bridle.
The bit is a piece of metal
that rests in the horse's mouth.
Reins are the leather straps
you hold in your hands.

Metal stirrups hang from the saddle.

Your feet go in the stirrups.

There are two main styles
of horseback riding.
They are English
and Western.
The tack for each
is a little different.

Are horses smart?

Horses have small brains,

but they are smart.

They can remember people, places,

and events for a long time.

They can understand some words.

What jobs can horses do?

Horses can do many jobs.

They help herd cattle and sheep
on ranches.

Police ride horses in many cities
because horses can go places cars can't.

Horses are ridden in sports
such as polo, hunting, and racing.

Some horses work in rodeos or circuses.

Horses even compete in the Olympics.

Who are some famous horses?

A palomino horse named Mr. Ed
was a famous actor in the 1960s.
He was the star of his own TV show.
The Lipizzaner stallions are a group
of white horses from Austria.
They have been trained
to perform tricks and dance in shows.

Secretariat was a famous racehorse.

He surprised everyone

by winning the Triple Crown.

That means he won three

important races in one year.

Horses are also featured

in popular books and movies

such as *Black Beauty* and *National Velvet*.

How can I learn to ride?

The best way to learn to ride a horse

is to go to riding school.

The first things you will learn

are how to get on and off a horse

and how to hold the reins.

Then you'll be taught how to

make a horse walk and stop.

Next you'll learn trotting and cantering.

After you do those well, you may

train to gallop and jump.

How do I tell a horse what I want it to do?

Use your voice, hands, legs,

and body to show your horse

what you want it to do.

Always speak softly when approaching

a horse, so you don't scare it.

The tone of your voice helps

your horse understand

what you want.

When you're on a horse and you want to
move your horse forward,
squeeze your legs against its sides.
Pull gently on the reins
to slow your horse.

Horses are beautiful to look at,

and fun to get to know.

Treat a horse well,

and once it gets to know you,

it will be a good friend.